B

L

I

N

D

Book IV in the

Series

By

E.W. Brooks

This is a work of fiction. The events and characters described herein are imaginary and are not intended to refer to specific places or living persons. The opinions expressed in the manuscript are solely the opinions or thoughts of the author. The author has represented and warranted full ownership and/or legal right to publish all the materials in this book.

This book may not be reproduced, transmitted, or stored in whole or in part by any means, including graphic, electronic, or mechanical without the express written consent of the author except in the case of brief quotations embodied in critical articles and reviews.

ISBN: 0692060227
ISBN-13: 978-0692060223

Preface

I was pretty much done with the Mafietta Series. My last venture wore me out and I went back to a nine to five. I love the work I do, but it didn't stop that quiet nudge from my first love.

It felt like I'd abandoned my baby and all the people who'd supported me over the last three years.

Then I had a producer tell me, "Mafietta is tainted." I think that was when I knew it was time for her return.

. . .and just like that, Clarke, Errol, and Mafietta are back.

Thank you, Mr. Producer, for waking the giant.

-   *E.W.*

Chapter 1 – Caught You Slippin

"Melissa and Edwina just grabbed 2 more boxes of cereal and another bag of chips. I'm gonna kill those girls when I get them home. They're running from aisle to aisle throwing stuff in the cart like they're crazy. They act like I'm made of money!"

"Is it food?" Arlen asked, smiling at Tesha.

"Yep, but you don't . . ."

Arlen placed his finger over Tesha's lips. "Then leave them alone. It's not like they're at Macy's. This is the grocery store, Babe." Arlen laughed as he threw two boxes of cereal into the cart.

Tesha had been trying to trim the grocery bill ever since Arlen put her on a budget. There was no more balling out once he came on the scene. He was a business analyst, and he was something special with those numbers. He'd done well with the stock market and helped turn a profit for Tesha too. She'd made enough money from the sale of her beauty salon to take care of herself and Edwina had her own money.

Arlen never knew who Edwina's father was, but he did know that two big dudes and sometimes a woman would drop by every couple of months to check on the girl. He also noticed that they always left a big wad of cash. Today was no different and Edwina knew it too. She saw Clarke and Black when they left the apartment.

She and Melissa ran down the aisle of the grocery store, grabbing two and three of all their favorite foods. They'd learned to get all of their stuff at the beginning of the month before all the money ran out.

Outside of paying into her own savings and brokerage accounts, Tesha was a horrible manager of money and the fat stacks of cash never lasted for thirty full days. Edwina got tired of going to school with no lunch money because Tesha had smoked it up or gone to the club one too many times. Instead of questioning her mother, Edwina learned to make a little money cleaning for the lady next door to fill in the gaps. She was young, but she knew better than to tell Arlen about the shortfalls. Tesha woke her daughter up with a belt the last time she asked Arlen for money. She cared more about Arlen's opinion of her than her daughter's empty stomach and Edwina knew it.

The two girls met Tesha and Arlen at the front of the store and they watched Tesha gasp as the total came to $357.15. Edwina knew her mother was already trying to figure out how to pay her weed man for the month and where she would pull the money from without Arlen noticing.

Arlen turned to give each of the young ladies a dollar to get a nick knack out of the vending machine. The girls ran ahead. Arlen and Tesha waited on the attendant to put the bags back in their cart, leaving them a few steps behind. The couple laughed as they rounded the front of the building. Tesha's smile faded and her heart raced as she spotted Clarke Bellow. She and Black were talking to Edwina and Melissa. She grimaced as he heard her daughter's conversation.

"No, Mrs. Clarke. Melissa gave me these. She said they didn't fit her, but I know better. She was just being nice."

"Really?" Clarke asked, raising an eyebrow at Tesha. "I thought sure your Mommy would have gotten you new shoes when school started."

Tesha rushed over to Edwina and placed her hands on her shoulders. She hoped to signal

8

Edwina to stop talking but found herself placing her hands over her daughter's mouth instead.

"What she means is – these are her play shoes," Tesha answered.

Melissa remembered Mrs. Clarke from her visits and continued for her friend, "Nuh uh because she wears them to school every day. Her other ones broke."

"They broke?" Clarke asked.

"Yep," Melissa continued. "Her feet started getting wet and wearing tape on your shoes is embarrassing, Mrs. Clarke, so I gave her mine. They're not that old. Look!" The child explained. "Now they don't pick on Edwina at school about her raggedy shoes anymore."

Clarke couldn't hide the tear that fell from her face as she felt the innocent and pure hearts of these children.

"Black, go grab a burner." Clarke ordered. Then without a word, the tall man with long dreadlocks vanished into the store.

"Ummm, Clarke, I need to get dinner started for the girls. We've gotta run."

"Hey girls, here's 5 bucks each. Let's see which one of you can use those claws and win that bear for me." Clarke bribed the small children. She smiled as they walked away in a deep debate as to which one of them would win the prize.

As soon as the girls were out of earshot, Clarke Bellow turned on her heels walked until she was within inches of Tesha's face.

"What the fuck have you been doing with that girl's money, Tesha?"

"I don't know what you mean, Clarke," she responded, trying to dodge the issue in front of her man, but Mafietta didn't care. It was time to put Tesha in her place and Arlen on notice.

"Bitch, don't play with me. With the money you get from Mandell's death and the money from Edwina's Godmother, she shouldn't wear the same underwear twice, so where is the money going Tesha?"

Arlen stood there, trying to absorb all the information just thrown in his lap. *How could she do this?* He thought. Finally, he found the courage to speak.

"Ma'am, I know you help to take care of Edwina, but how do you expect Tesha to do all of these things on the fifteen hundred dollars you bring every couple of months. You're asking way too much," Arlen said, sticking out his chest.

"Oh, so not only are you a trifling bitch, you're a lying one too, and you wonder why no one will marry you," Clarke said looking at the woman. "Tesha gets five thousand dollars a month for Edwina in addition to living rent free. The two of you should be able to make up the difference without taking from this baby."

"Five thousand dollars a month?!?" Arlen asked, obviously perturbed.

"Isn't that right Tesha?" Clarke asked her opponent now pinned to the mat.

"Um, yeah, but we really gotta go. Alright?" Tesha pleaded with her eyes in hopes Clarke would give her a break. She didn't have to worry long because Black soon emerged with a small cellular phone.

"I just activated it, Boss," he advised Clarke.

"Great, I'm gonna go give this to Edwina, and that'll give you two time to load the car. How does that sound?" Clarke advised.

"Let's get these groceries home," Tesha said, pushing the cart as Arlen followed silently, shaking his head.

***

Clarke held Edwina's hand as they walked to the car.

"Baby, if you ever wanna go shopping or get your hair or nails done, hit me up. I'll make sure your mother takes you."

"Thank you, Mrs. Clarke, but I don't wanna get into trouble."

"Baby, you are a little lady. You have to take care of yourself. I'm sure your mother won't mind and if she does or if she is too busy, I'll send Mr. Black to take you. Got it?" Clarke asked as she patted Edwina and Melissa on the nose.

"Don't worry Mrs. Clarke. If she won't tell you, I will," Melissa answered smiling.

"I'm glad to hear that little lady. I gotta run, so yawl take care of yourselves and call me if you need anything." Clarke smiled. She held their hands and walked them back to Tesha, Arlen, and the car.

Clarke opened the door and looked at Tesha through squinted eyes.

"Hey, Tesha. Let me holla at you for a second."

"Sure thing, Clarke," she said as a thousand possible scenarios played in her head.

Tesha exited the car as Clarke began to walk toward her all black SUV. The embarrassed mother followed. Black opened the door as Clarke entered. He stood there waiting for Tesha. She entered slowly then the doors closed behind her.

"Have you lost your fucking mind, Tesha?" Clarke asked.

"When I told you to take care of that girl, that's what I meant. I didn't mean for you to half ass everything. She should be wearing name brand shit. Nothing less. You got that. I know what kind of money I give you, and I should have told your boy toy about the $10,000 you really get every month, but I decided to let you live. I've also heard how you can't stay away from the weed man, so let me make this easy for you.

Clarke knocked on the window, and Black opened the door. "Put the word out, Mafietta and The Port City Kings have an issue with anyone who sells to this bitch, especially since she doesn't know how to take care of home first."

Tesha opened her mouth, but she saw the look on Clarke's face just before the words found the strength to leave her lips.

"Bitch, if I were you, I'd get your low-class ass out of my car before I slap the stupid outta you – and the next time you touch that baby for some bullshit like she ate too many chips; I'm gonna see you."

Tesha stepped out of the Suburban and headed back to her own car.

Clarke spoke as Tesha walked away. "You'd better be sure to take care of those ballet lessons for Edwina and Melissa, but let's do it before you make that Lexus car note this month."

Tesha tried to hold her head up as she headed to her family.

"What was all that about?" Arlen asked.

"Just mind your fuckin business right now, Nosey," Tesha answered trying to hide the bite that hissed through her words.

Arlen knew something was amiss but decided not to press Tesha in front of the kids.

"Guess what Mrs. Clarke told me, Mommy." Edwina smiled.

That's when Tesha lost it.

"That woman is not your mother. I am your motherfuckin', Momma. Not her. You have to listen to me. Do you understand that? You listen to me. Don't nobody give a damn about that little Trac phone she gave you either. You are mine. Do you hear me? You are mine and she can't outrank me. Nope, she can't outrank me."

Melissa and Edwina looked at each other, both perplexed by Tesha's comments.

Arlen turned up the radio and watched as the girls danced around in the back seat. Tesha was pissed, but deep in his heart of hearts - Arlen knew Edwina having a cell phone was the best thing for her. Finally, someone would hold Tesha's feet to the fire, and he could be free of her without having to worry about Edwina.

Clarke sighed loudly as Black started the car. He smiled, waiting on Clarke to begin her rant.

"Can you believe this shit? This bitch is taking that baby's money."

Black laughed. "Did you really think that broad would spend all that money on that little girl? She's way too hood booger for that."

"I'm not gonna lose that baby to the streets and Tesha's bullshit. Got it?"

"I hear ya, Boss, but we got bigger fish to fry."

"Why are you telling me and not Errol?" Clarke asked.

"You know Errol doesn't do disrespect and the flagrant bullshit this Armon nigga is pulling is on level ten."

"How in the world can you fuck up sitting at home and collecting a check? We made that motherfucker a millionaire. What is his problem?"

17

"He says he can make more money on the street. He went underground and shit. He even talked to JayDee."

"How did you find out?"

"JayDee called me for the green light because he knew Armon was with the Port City Kings."

"Get his ass on the phone right now."

Armon answered after two rings. "King of the World on the line. What's up?"

"King of the World, huh? Well, since we're throwing around titles, should I remind you of mine?"

"The entire city knows who you are, Mafietta," he responded with an attitude.

"Cut the bullshit, Dude. If you know who I am, then why the FUCK are you testing me, Armon? I made you a very rich man, legally. Why do you have such a problem collecting a damned check like someone respectable? Why is there always some shit in the game with you?"

"Yo, Clarke. Why you so heated?"

"Why am I so heated," Clarke seethed. "I made you rich. You are set for life and you don't know what to do with yourself, do you?"

"Clarke, man I feel naked out here. I am a man. I should be doing something, not just sitting around. I'm bored as hell."

Clarke laughed. "I hear ya, but we gotta stay on the straight and narrow. Find something you love and we'll find someone to show you how to make money with it, LEGALLY."

"Sounds like you're shooting me some Oprah Winfrey, aha moment bullshit." He snapped.

"Curse me again and I'll slap the shit out of you, but don't worry. I have something in mind. Come by tomorrow and we can chat it up."

"Thanks, Clarke."

"No worries, but don't ever go to the streets before coming to me."

"I gotcha Boss Lady. You're coming in loud and clear."

"I betta be." Clarke smiled. "See ya tomorrow." She looked over at Black as he shook his head and ended the call.

"So now, I get to be a shrink, too?" Clarke asked.

"These guys have no idea what to do without the streets. Eventually, you're gonna have to find a way to keep them all busy. Hustling is all they know."

"That may be so, but we have to teach them to hustle another way. We didn't spend 5 years distancing ourselves from that shit to fall back into it," Clarke preached.

"So, what you gone do, Boss?" Black asked.

"Not sure yet," Clarke responded, "but I'll think of something."

Clarke spent the rest of the drive home considering ways to keep the Port City Kings busy. These men needed businesses to run. They'd proven their ability to manage employees, keep up with inventory and handle the books. Most of them were smart. They just needed to be challenged.

Clarke's thought shifted as the car stopped. She grabbed the box of cupcakes and headed in to greet her family. Errol Magnus ran to her, "Mommy. Mommy. You got the cupcakes?"

"I sure did, Sugar Lump. You were good all week like you promised, plus these cupcakes are the best in town."

EM smiled back at her. "Yep, they sure are. Mommy, can I take one to Daddy?"

"Sure, Baby, but be sure to grab one for Uncle Admiral too. If you don't, he'll bite yours."

"I know, Mommy. Last time he almost ate the whole thing." The little man complained with a face so serious it made Clarke laugh.

"Wait, I'll just take one, and you can take the rest into the man cave with your father."

The doting mother grabbed the treat and watched as her son ran to share his goodies with his Dad and Uncle Ad. Life was good and she wanted to keep it that way.

***

"Did you see those numbers, Man?" Errol asked his brother.

"I have to give it to that wife of yours. She is a fucking financial genius. Who knew that going legit could be this profitable?"

"How is everything else going?" Errol half whispered.

"You're getting mighty brave talking about that here," Admiral warned and his hunches served correct. The heavy office door began to creak and open slowly.

"Hi, Daddy. Hi, Uncle Ad. I got cupcakes," EM screamed as he ran and hugged his father's legs.

Admiral reached for the box. "You know you can't hide this from her forever, right?"

Errol scratched his head. "I know. I just have to find a way to tell her."

"That should be easy, Daddy. Mommy says all you have to do is tell the truth, and it makes everything easier. Plus, that's what Jesus would do, right Daddy?" The child asked as he looked at his father with eyes of admiration.

"You are so right EM." Errol told his son as he wrestled with the difference between his words and his actions.

"You don't think she'll leave me, do you, Bro?" Errol asked his older brother and counselor.

"Nah, y'all been through too much together, but she'll probably whip your ass." Admiral laughed.

"Ain't no woman besides Momma gonna whip me," Errol smiled.

"Do you remember who you married? You know she's gonna fire that ass up."

"Yeah, but we couldn't just leave it all on the table like that. There was too much money to be made and besides, we're staying away from all the hard shit. This is just weed."

"You don't have to convince me, Brother," Admiral said, throwing up his hands. The brothers turned as they heard a knock at the door.

"Come in," Errol ordered.

"Houston, we have a problem," Black reported.

"What is it now?" Admiral asked.

"It's Clarke. She saw that woman Tesha at the store, and she hasn't been taking care of the little one, so Clarke went ballistic. She even had me buy the little girl a burner phone. I know she's Mafietta and all, but she may be taking this one a little too far."

"You know how headstrong she is. She's too passionate and way too invested. Keep an eye on her okay. Something about that Tesha makes my skin crawl. I don't trust her." Errol responded

"Gotcha, Boss," Black replied.

"Wass up Mr. Black?" The youngster asked with a smile.

"Hey Lil' Man. How's it going?" Black asked as he poked the smiling toddler.

"Yo, don't touch me, Mr. Black. I'm fresh today." The little one returned as the room roared with laughter.

Chapter 3 - Take Care of Home

Errol Bellow had been working double time to keep his operation away from Clarke. She'd worked so hard to clean their images and make the team legitimate cash that he didn't have the heart to tell her the crew was still running weed.

Clarke could never wrap her mind around the amount of weed the team smoked. Finding an outsider who could keep up with their demands became challenging. Then with all the snitching and bitching, it was just easier to have his own supply. Once the old heads hit his stuff, they only wanted herb straight from the island, and before Errol Bellow knew it, he was thrust back into the deep.

It came so naturally to him that he didn't even recognize the numbers he was pulling until Clarke ran across an extra $25,000 in the safe. He was trying to stay small, but he was growing faster than he wanted. While all of his generals would be straight for life, those who were lower on the totem pole still had to hustle for their money. Those were the people you had to watch. Hungry babies and empty cabinets had ways of making a man do some crazy things.

His small enterprise maintained the status quo. He was, in fact, helping his wife. He just had to tell her.

"Hey, Babe. What's on your mind? She asked as she found Errol staring out of his office window."

"Oh, nothing. I was just taking a walk down memory lane."

"Uh oh," Clarke responded jokingly. "What's up?"

"What do you mean?" He asked smiling.

"You know what I'm talking about. There is something that always pulls you to that side of things. There is all this legal money on the table, and you can't seem to be okay with making it the straight way. I just can't wrap my mind around that."

"I can't explain it, Clarke. I guess there is something to be said for power and influence. They are drugs themselves and what can I say? They both have me hooked pretty badly."

"You still take care of families. You are still Elder. You are still the man. Why do you need to be on top again?"

"I need something that demands my attention daily. I need something to run. Something I control and direct."

"What do you have in mind?" Clarke asked.

"I'm not sure yet, Babe. All I know is that this idea of yours is gonna have to change the mentality of a lot of folks and it takes more than money to do that, so we're gonna have to put some real thought into this campaign."

"Sounds good to me. Lena and her father will be here in a few weeks. We should sit down and map out the next few moves while she's here."

"Are you sure about her?" Errol asked.

"Yeah, she's pretty solid. She says what she means and that makes her different than most."

"Can we trust her for this next level shit, though?" He asked.

"What other family has the money to match ours? We can find a lot of smart people out here with great ideas. Some of them may even be better than ours, but it doesn't mean a lot if they can't put up the money it takes to make the dream a reality."

"So, this is just strategic alignment?" Errol asked, finally understanding his wife's relationship to his weed connect.

Lena promised not to share her and Errol's dealings with Clarke because she was so hell bent on getting The Kings out of the business altogether. Errol was afraid this kind of news would send her packing and piss Magnus off, but he knew a conversation would be needed sooner than later. If his packages got any larger, there would be no way to hide them from Magnus or anyone else for that matter. It was time to come clean.

"Yep. We are really working hard to find a way to employ more people. It bothers me that we left so many soldiers out there hanging. It is only a matter of time before they come gunning for us. They know who cut off their supply. We gotta get ahead of that," Clarke responded with a look of consternation on her face.

Errol smiled. He just may have a way to lay this on Clarke without her boiling over. He rolled a joint and inhaled deeply.

"I wish you'd quit with that shit. We have a son. What are you going to tell him if he sees you?"

Errol laughed. "You should try it. You'd loosen up a bit," he joked.

"Well, if you were on your job. I wouldn't be so tense, Mr. Bellow," Clarke flirted.

"Oh no. That's you with that, 'I don't want him to hear us crap.' You know I want what you got," Errol said pulling his wife close and planting her with a kiss just before EM came running in the door.

"Ooooh, yawl kissing." The toddler joked.

"See what I mean," Clarke laughed.

**

"What do you mean he's running drugs again?" Magnus screamed into the phone. He tapped the desk with his massive diamond and emerald studded pinky ring as his informant brought him up to speed on his son-in-law's latest venture.

"Thanks, man. Good lookin," Magnus returned before slamming down the phone. "My daughter is gonna kill him," Magnus mumbled to himself.

"Rodney!" He yelled to his right-hand man standing just outside the door.

"Yeah, Boss," he answered.

"Bring me my damned car. I have something to take care of." Magnus said as he rose from his chair and put on his blazer before heading to the door.

"You okay, Boss?" Rodney asked.

"I will be," he returned as he put his Glock in its holster and turned off the light.

***

Errol stepped away as he saw the call come in from Admiral. He cleverly distanced himself from Clarke and EM. Clarke would understand, he thought, but something deep within him said that was a lie.

The Port City King closed the office door behind him as his wife and child headed to the kitchen for ice cream.

"I thought I told you never to call me about this shit when I was at home," Errol whispered loudly into the receiver. He knew the loves of his life would be coming through the door in minutes with a snack. He had to handle this quickly.

"Shut up, Boy. You're the one hustling and too afraid to tell your wife," Admiral laughed.

"If you weren't my brother . . ." Errol returned. "What is so urgent that we have to talk about this now?"

"Your shipment is gone," one brother informed the other.

"Hell, you mean it's gone?"

"I got here, and Lester said someone picked it up already."

"Who in the world would test me that way?" Errol asked his brother.

"Think, man. Who runs the Port?"

"Magnus?" He asked in disbelief.

"Yep," Admiral laughed. "You just got jacked by your own father-in-law."

"Damn!" Errol said as his fist pounded the wall. "I'll take care of it."

"You'd better. You have a lot of people waiting on that."

"They're just gonna have to wait. Does Clarke know yet?"

"Know what, Baby?" Clarke asked as she and EM opened the door with a bowl of hot fudge ice cream covered with sprinkles made just for him.

"I'll tell you later," Errol said, pointing at EM and shaking his head.

Errol let out a sigh of relief as his wife relented and began eating from her own bowl. He knew the conversation wasn't over, but at least it bought him some time.

Chapter 4 – We Don't Keep Secrets

Clarke smiled as she pulled her pot roast from the oven. The smell spread through the house as the happy wife hummed to herself. The doorbell rang just as she sat the pan on the counter.

"Can you get the door, Babe?" She screamed, hoping Errol could hear her.

"I got it," Errol returned as he and EM ran to the door to welcome her father.

"What's up, Magnus?" Errol asked, trying to remain calm.

Magnus reached out to hug his son-in-law and whispered into his ear. "If my grandson weren't in here, I'd lay your lying ass out on this floor." He hissed before quickly pushing Errol away as EM grabbed his leg.

"Hey, Grandpa." The jovial boy almost yelled. "I missed you. I got stronger since last time. Let me show you. Feel my muscles."

Magnus and Errol laughed as the boy's grandfather reached down to feel EM's arm.

Clarke walked in with a smile covering her face as she watched her family's interaction.

"Hey, Daddy," she said as she reached to hug her father.

"Hey, Baby," he returned. "Is that a roast, I smell?"

"You know it. Let me get back to these pots. We eat in twenty minutes," Clarke said before turning to head to the kitchen.

"EM, your granddaddy needs a new painting for the wall in his office. Can you take care of that for me?"

"Sure thing, Grandpa. I am gonna start on it now," the little boy said as he ran toward his play room.

Magnus began to walk toward Errol's office. The head of the Port City Kings bowed his head and followed his father-in-law into the room. Suddenly the massive office wasn't his anymore. Errol watched as his father-in-law and mentor went to his bar and poured two glasses of cognac. Magus took his cup, handed Errol one and went to the largest seat in the room – the one behind the desk. Magnus was punkin' Errol and he knew it, but the OG had to prove a point.

"Grab us a couple of cigars," Magnus instructed before watching shaky hands grab two cigars from the humidor.

The men clipped their ends and each took their time lighting the Cubans. Errol downed his shot, and Magnus knew he was ready to talk.

"Is there anything you need to tell me, Son?"

"Other than the fact that someone jacked my weed shipment, nah Pops. There's nothing."

"Is that the way you wanna handle this?" Magnus asked as his temper rose.

"I'm not sure what you want me to say, Magnus. You know I smoke. What was I supposed to do, buy lower grade shit from someone else? Nah, man. I wanted the real ganja."

"Don't play with me, boy. I just fell on fifty pounds of that shit."

"It ain't mine!" Errol belted.

The look on Magnus' face told the man that he'd better get to explaining, and fast.

"I know this sounds crazy, but I only ordered half that amount. The rest of it doesn't belong to me. I have another ten coming in a week, but only half of that is mine, Magnus."

"So, are you telling me someone tried to bring something through my port and not tell me?"

"That's exactly what I am saying."

"Who would be dumb enough to do some stupid shit like that?" Magnus asked as he took a deep pull on his cigar.

"I think we should start with this little young cat named Armon. Black told me about the eager little motherfucker last week, but I had no idea he could pull off anything that heavy."

"You don't get it. There are much larger implications here. There are only certain people who even have the access and ability to get things through."

"So, what are you saying, Magnus?" Errol asked, leaning forward in his chair.

"Julius St. James is the only man connected enough to me to do this."

Magnus watched as his son-in-law fidgeted in his seat.

"What is it that you should be telling me, Errol?"

"It's Lena. She was my connect. It wasn't her father."

"You are one stupid motherfucker, son. My daughter is going to kill you."

"I know Magnus. She really doesn't know Lena St. James. She just thinks she does."

"You have to get out of this shit for two reasons. My daughter will REALLY kill you if she finds out and if you don't get this shit away from my grandson, I'm gonna kill you myself. Have you forgotten what Clarke went through laying in that damned hospital bed and we not knowing if she would ever open her eyes again or not? You vowed to protect her and you aren't doing that right now. You are putting both my daughter and grandson in danger all because you are too prideful to buy weed from someone else."

"It's not just that, Magnus."

"I don't care what the fuck it is. You have one week to get this shit together or I'm taking my daughter and my grandson."

"How dare you threaten to take my family? You know I love them more than life."

"Shut your dumb ass up, boy," Magnus growled. "We don't keep secrets in this family, not after everything we've been through. After dinner, I am gonna take my grandson out for an afternoon in the park, and you are gonna come clean with my daughter – today."

"Come on Magnus. Don't make me do that."

The OG pounded the desk with his fist. "You nasty nigga. You bring my daughter in this shit after I spent her entire life protecting her from it. Then you partner with a woman she considers a friend, and you don't tell her. I'd consider that a major violation. So, let me make this clear, you fix this shit, or someone is gonna find your black ass, burnt to a crisp in the back of somebody's trunk. Don't mistake my likeness for you - for love. My daughter comes first, so you tell my baby the truth today and let her deal with you. But know this, if you lay a hand on her, I'll cut it off and watch you bleed the fuck out. You went too far this time, Errol. We don't keep secrets in this family."

Magnus threw back his shot and slammed the glass on the desk so hard it broke. Then he left Errol to figure out how to tell his wife what he'd been up to as he went upstairs to check on EM and his painting.

Chapter 5 – You Did What

Dinner was super awkward. There were the normal smiles and polite conversation, but something was off. Clarke could feel it, so much so, she was relieved when it was over.

"That was great as usual, Baby."

"Thanks, Daddy," Clarke replied.

"Yep, now I am gonna take my grandson, and we're going to hang out for a while."

"Yayy, Grandpa! Can we go to that place and get ice cream with tons of sprinkles again, pleasssse?"

"Dad, is that why my son is always so eager to go places with you?"

"Of course not." Magnus smiled. "You hang out with Grandpa because you love him don't you, EM?"

"Yep, Grandpa. That's right. We got that Williams blood, Mommy. We stick together," Clarke laughed at her baby, who wasn't much of a baby anymore.

"I'll have him back around eight," Magnus said as he rose and kissed his daughter on her forehead. "I think you and your husband need to talk."

Clarke's nose flared as she watched her husband drop his head. *What the fuck has he been up to?* She wondered to herself.

EM ran to Clarke and hugged his Mommy. He did the same with Errol. Then he and Magnus were out of the door.

Clarke poured herself a glass of wine and her husband a glass of cognac. "Now what is it that you have to tell me?" She asked before taking a sip of the numbing liquid.

"It's not as bad as you think."

"Then that's great, but let me be the judge of that."

"Your father ganked my last shipment from the port," Errol admitted reluctantly.

"What the fuck did you just say?" Clarke asked as the crystal wine glass crashed to the floor. Clarke was in such shock that she missed the table entirely.

Errol proceeded, not sure how his wife would take the news. "I started smoking again, and the shit here was whack, so I started ordering stuff from home."

"How much?"

"Only 10 pounds, Babe."

"10 fucking pounds Errol?" Clark screamed. "You can't be smoking that much weed."

"No, I don't, but the crew does."

Clarke picked up a piece of the broken glass stem and pointed it at her husband.

"Boy, don't play with me."

"It all started when I . . ."

"Cut the bullshit, Errol," Clarke loudly spoke as she threw the glass toward his face.

"Fine, Mafietta. I'm selling weed again."

"You dumb motherfucker. Why would you do that? You have more money than you can spend in a lifetime."

"I know, Baby but I can get it so cheap and green from the island is ten times better than the bullshit these two-bit hustlers are out here spraying with shit. I wanted the real thing, so I got it. Then when others found out I had the good shit, they wanted it too and before you know it I was selling weed again, but not like before. This time, it was only to other Kings."

Clarke was so shocked. She could hardly speak. "We worked so hard to separate ourselves from that shit. How could you do this?" Tears began to fall from her face and and her fist pounded the table. Errol's heart broke. He loved his wife, but he couldn't escape this life no matter how he tried.

"Where did you get it from?" Clarke asked.

"From home," the guilty husband responded.

"That's not what I'm asking, and you know it. Who did you get it from?"

"Baby, it doesn't matter it was all harmless."

Before Errol knew it, Clarke had a piece of the broken glass at his neck. "I did a lot of shit because I loved you. I became someone I don't even recognize to protect you and then you lie to me. I have blood all over my hands because of YOU, and this is the fucking thanks I get. Who the fuck sent it?"

"Lena," Errol almost whispered.

"Lena, who?" Clarke asked, unable to believe it could be her new acquaintance.

"Lena St. James," He responded as he finally found the courage to look his wife in the eye.

The force came so fast, it made his head spin. Clarke had slapped spit from his mouth.

"You find the one person who is supposed to be creating legal opportunities with me, and then you have her ship you weed through my Daddy's port, and you don't even tell me. I've never lied to you. NEVER. Then you go and do some dumb shit like this with a woman who calls herself my friend and you don't think to tell me. You have me looking like a fool among the people I do business with."

"No, baby. That wasn't my intention."

"I don't give a damn about your intention. I care about the truth," Clarke cried.

"Baby, don't cry. You know I hate it when you cry. Come here, Clarke."

"No, you know I wanted a clean slate, but don't worry, Baby. I know how to fix this."

Errol's big eyes filled with water and he attempted to open his mouth, but Clarke quickly put the glass stem back to his neck.

"Get the fuck outta my house."

"What do you mean, Baby? You're making this bigger than it is."

"I almost died behind this shit. It could have cost us EM's life too, and all you can say is I'm making this about more than it is. I won't have our lives endangered again because of you and this nigga shit. You have money, but that's not enough. You have a beautiful family that loves you and that's not enough either. So, since you can't respect and appreciate your family, it's time you be without us. NOW GET THE FUCK OUT OF MY HOUSE!" Clarke screamed.

Errol rose as his did his anger. "You can't throw me out of my own house."

"I bet the fuck I can. I'm going to the store, and your lying ass had better be gone by the time I get back. I love you, but I love my son more. Get your shit and get the fuck out," Clarke almost choked on her words, but she continued. "I can't stand the sight of you. You put my baby in danger all over again. What the fuck kinda father are you? That boy loves you and look what you do. You create a life that could kill us both after we've already been freed from it. You are a special kind of stupid and now you can go live in the damned street with all the trash you can't seem to get away from."

"How long?"

"Until I say you can come back."

"Baby, you don't mean that. It's only weed."

"Only weed. You still don't fucking get it. We just started a foundation in the city to help young men leave gangs, and here you come to ruin it all. We have a name in this city. I have a name, and I won't let you tarnish it. Fuck that. You don't get to put us at risk again. You don't get to do that. So get your black ass the fuck outta my house."

Errol could see there would be no reasoning with his wife. He needed to get out of there before she really flipped out but everything in him wanted to stay and love away all the pain he'd caused her. She'd been more than good to him and she didn't deserve the shit he put her through, even if he didn't mean any harm.

The now estranged husband packed slowly, hoping his wife would mount the stairs to the bedroom they shared. If she came upstairs, he knew he had a chance, but she didn't. She was too hurt. She watched in pain as her husband headed for the door with an overnight bag in tow. Tears welled in her eyes, but she refused to let another one fall. She gulped down a glass of cognac as Errol closed the door behind him.

Now she had to deal with Lena and somebody had to go to the store.

Admiral peeked out of the window as a familiar figure approached. It was Errol. He rushed to open the door and meet his brother. Immediately, he knew what was wrong.

"Lil' Stupid, I'll call you back." The uncle advised his nephew before hanging up the phone.

"What's wrong, Lil Bro?" Admiral asked, trying to sound supportive when deep inside he already knew Clarke had thrown Errol out.

"You already know," he said as he dropped his bag on the floor and plopped down on the sofa.

"How did she find out?" Admiral asked.

"Her father."

"Magnus ratted you out?"

"Nope, but he "politely" encouraged me to snitch on myself."

"And you did it?" Admiral asked with a puzzled look on his face.

"Call me crazy. I have a real respect for the man and after everything that happened when

Clarke was shot and EM was born, I can't say I blame him."

"So, what are you gonna do?"

"Shit. What you think I'm gone do?" Errol asked with a smile. "I'm gonna get my family back. I love Clarke. I love my son," Errol said as a tear fell from his eye.

"You'd better get this shit fixed and fast, Bro. How can I help?"

***

Clarke paced the floor as she watched Tia, the housekeeper, clean the wall mirror.

"Are you okay Ms. Bellow? And when will Mr. Bellow be returning?" She asked with a concerned look on her face.

"Yes, I'm fine and I'll let you know, thanks," Clarke answered before leaving the room. She wasn't prepared for questions about Errol's whereabouts. The only thing on her mind was getting to Lena St. James.

***

Lena rushed to grab her cell as she heard it ringing.

"What's up Clarke?" She asked.

"Nothing much, I just want to double tap and make sure you'll be here next month. I've been researching some of your business ventures, and I have a couple of questions for you."

"Which ventures do you have questions about?"

"Just one," Clarke returned.

"Oh, that's too easy. Which one?" She answered.

"The one you have with my husband," Clarke returned.

"Excuse me?" Lena asked as she cleared her throat.

"We've been able to make a ton of money together, but that means nothing right now. Don't test me when it comes to my family, Lena."

"I'm not sure what you're talking about," she responded.

"I'm talking about the marijuana you just sent to my husband."

"Ummm, not sure what you're talking about," Lena answered.

"Lena, this is not a fucking game."

"I understand that Clarke, but it didn't come from me."

"Then who the hell else could it have come from? If you didn't send it, who did?"

"I'm not sure, but I will certainly get on the case for you."

"If you didn't do this, we're in more danger than I thought. I gotta run, but let me know if you find out anything."

"Will do, Clarke. Be safe out there. I'll see you in a few of weeks."

Clarke didn't even say goodbye. She just hung up, and so did the maid downstairs. Tia, stepped outside to have a cigarette, but she grabbed her phone.

"Hey, Boss. We have a problem. Clarke just called Lena St. James and she say that ganja didn't come from her."

"What?" A voice screamed from the other side of the phone. "Who the hell sent it, then? Who have I been talking to?" The man asked, obviously perturbed.

"I can't say, Sir. I'm on it, though."

"Thanks, Tia."

"No problem, Boss," the maid said as she ashed out the cigarette and threw the butt in the sand filled bucket.

***

Tesha bammed on the door, but no one came to open it. "Armon!" She screamed, but still no answer. Finally, she'd had enough and decided to try the door knob. Her instincts proved her right as she found the young man sitting at his kitchen table with a bottle of Hennessy and a blunt.

"OH, so you weren't gonna open the door?" Tesha asked.

"I didn't know who it was, and I gotta lot on my mind, so I didn't ask. OK?"

Tesha picked up the shot glass and swallowed the warm liquid before grabbing the spliff from Armon's hand.

"Where's my weed, Lil' Nigga?" She asked.

"About that . . ."

"What the fuck you mean, about that? Do you know how much money I gave your little ass? Eight hundred dollars times two pounds is $1600, and that's what I gave you, so where's my shit?"

"We had a slight problem."

"What do you mean, problem?" Tesha asked as she blew smoke from her nose.

"I verified that the smoke made it to the Port, but there is no trace of it after that. I called Lester to inquire, and all he said was I needed to talk to Magnus, but I ain't for doing that shit."

"Why the hell not? He ain't nobody."

"Girl, you must be stupid. That's Mafietta's Daddy, and nothing comes in this city without him approving it. If he says no, it doesn't happen, and it looks like he said no, Lil Lady."

"Damn!" Tesha said as she hit Armon's blunt again. "Got any more of this stuff?" She asked.

"Yeah, it's in the back."

"Go get it. I wanna see it. I gotta cop some."

Armon looked at Tesha, knowing she was asking him to break the first and second rule of hustling. She was asking him to sell her something from his home, and he hadn't bagged it yet, so it was still shaped like a brick with the corners chiseled away.

"Oh, yeah. I want all that. Let me smell it," Tesha said with a smile.

"You got enough money for this, Tesha. This is all I got."

"Hell yeah, I got money," she replied as Armon reluctantly handed her his private stash.

"Thanks," Tesha laughed as she placed the package in her purse.

"What the hell you mean, thanks? I want my bread," Armon said as he rose and began to approach Tesha.

"The way I see it, Armon – you owe me one more pound or my $800 back and I really don't give a fuck how you get it, but I want my money or my green. If you don't fix this, you're gonna have a bigger problem than me."

"Take the shit. You'll need me before I need you. I heard Mafietta banned the streets from selling to your ass anyway. I see you forgot to tell me that, but it's okay, though. That'll last you what, 2 or 3 weeks. That ain't shit. You'll be back, but for now, you can get the fuck out of my apartment before I call Mafietta on that ass."

"I ain't scared of her," Tesha bragged.

"Well, you damned sure should be," Armon laughed.

Tesha broke a piece of bark from the brick and handed it to Armon. "Here. Now, I'm not a total bitch, but I gotta split."

Armon watched as Tesha closed the door behind her.

"She just fucked up," he laughed. "She'd better make that last."

Chapter 7 – The Other Side of the Coin

Reshaunda Teal looked at herself in the mirror. She smiled and for a split second, she saw her sister. Suddenly, her happy morning turned into the beginning of one of those days. She put down her toothbrush and turned off the sink. She never even brushed her teeth. Instead, she grabbed a blunt and plopped down on her sofa. She flipped through several television stations and stopped when she saw it. It was a commercial promoting The Village. It sounded like a pretty cool place and besides, the teens in the city needed something positive to do.

Reshaunda nodded her head in approval as she agreed with the mission of the organization.

"Are you fucking kidding me?" Reshaunda screamed with her eyes frozen on the words "Sponsored by the Mafietta Movement" as she grabbed her cell phone.

"Hello," the young man answered.

"What's up Armon?"

"Well, I got some good news, and I got some bad news. Which do you want first?"

"Give it to me straight, Armon. What's wrong?"

"Your shipment got jacked."

"What the fuck do you mean, my shipment got jacked?" The woman asked as she began to lose her temper.

"It didn't make it past the port," He explained. "I can only track it to Lester. It got to him, but no trace after that. That probably means Magnus has it."

"Who the fuck is Magnus?" Reshaunda asked.

"Don't act like you don't remember. He is Mafietta's Dad, but he runs this city. He's usually pretty fair, so you should speak to him."

"Why the fuck should I speak to him when I know he, his daughter, and her husband had something to do with my sister's death," She answered, trying to control her emotions.

"Yo, you didn't tell me you had all of these other issues going on. Who is your sister?" Armon asked.

"Deshaunda Teal was my sister. Folks called her Dee. We're twins. Well, at least we were," Reshaunda answered slowly.

"Oh, hell no. You shoulda told me that up front. Those are the people you don't wanna fuck with. I'm out, Ma'am. I thought you were some nice voice I could make a lot of money with, but I didn't sign up for all of this," Armon answered.

"Look, you scary nigga. This ain't the time for that faint-hearted shit. We're in this together whether you like it or not." Reshaunda answered.

"No, you look, it takes big bucks to battle on their level. I just don't know that I wanna rock with you like that – not when my life is at stake."

"Don't underestimate me. Tell me what you need."

"I need bodies. I need protection. You're asking me to go to war for you, and I've never even met you. Hell no. Let's start with a meeting. I wanna see you tomorrow and enough with all this secret - I can't even have your number shit. Text me your number and I'll text you the place." Armon smirked before hanging up on Reshaunda.

He quickly dialed his homeboy, Stacy. "Yo, my hitta. We're back on. Get the crew together and ride through."

"Oh, shit. Hell yeah. Give me about 30 minutes and we'll be there," Stacy answered quickly.

Armon smiled as he thought, *this Lil Lady could put the gang back on before the Kings ever see me coming.*

***

"Mommy, where's Daddy?" EM asked as he rushed through the door.

"He's not here, Baby. He went to Uncle Admiral's house."

"When is he coming back? I got him a cookie," the young boy asked.

"I'm not sure, Baby. Uncle Ad is not feeling well, so your Dad had to go take care of him."

"Ok, call him," the little one persisted.

"Huh?" Clarke asked as her father looked on, trying to hide his smile.

"Well, we know where he got that from," Magnus joked.

Clarke quickly dialed Errol's number and handed the small child the phone.

"Hey, Daddy. Whatcha doing?"

"I'm about to go play soccer with your Uncle Admiral. How was your trip with Grandpa?"

"Soccer? I don't think that's good. Mommy said Uncle Ad was sick so you gotta take better care of him than that. You two need soup. I'm gonna tell Mommy to get you some. Hold on." EM looked so very concerned as the passed the phone to his Mom and whispered, "They need soup, Mommy."

Clarke had to laugh. She took the receiver and spoke quickly to her husband. "I'll get you the soup, but I gotta go. Daddy is here."

"Baby, I wanna come home."

"No, that isn't the best kind. No, No, No. You should just stay there and take it," Clarke answered, trying to save face in front of her son.

"I'm coming right now."

"No, Errol. I don't think that's a good idea."

"I just want to fix this, and I can't do that if I'm not at home with my family."

"I'd like to have had you do that in the beginning, and then we wouldn't be here, now would we?"

"I'm sorry, Clarke. I can fix this. Don't go all Mafietta on me. I'm coming home. I'm coming for my family."

"It doesn't really work like that. You have to heat it up first. You can't give it to him cold." Clarke answered, hoping EM couldn't understand.

"I'm coming home, Clarke, and that's that."

"Try it, Errol," Clarke hissed. "I think Mafietta may just have to make an appearance."

"You do what you have to and so will I. Let me speak to my son."

"Don't test me, boy."

"No, don't you test me. I told you how I felt about family before we were married. You've had time to cool off. Now, I'm coming home."

Clarke knew when she was defeated. She handed the phone to her son.

"What's going on, Baby?" Magnus whispered as EM talked with his Dad about the movie he wanted to watch during movie night.

"I called Lena, and she says she hasn't sent anything."

"Do you believe her?" Her father, Magnus asked.

"She sounded pretty straight up. She even offered to help me get to the bottom of things."

"That means we have a problem and that man needs to be home."

"No, Daddy. He promised me."

"Yeah, I know, but this could be bad, Clarke. You need him around."

"No, I don't."

"Clarke, I know you're strong, and no one can take that from you, but you have to know when to sit down. This is Errol's little red wagon. It's time you let him pull it. No one can fault you if you decide to let him take the lead on this one. He can handle it, but in the meantime, get the band back together. We're in red alert."

"Tia," Clarke yelled.

The housekeeper came running, "Yes, Mrs. Bellow."

"I need you to go to the grocery store and buy three of all the things EM likes to snack on and even the sometimes stuff. We're gonna have a family staycation and I want him to have everything he needs."

"Yes, Mrs. Bellow," Tia answered as she headed back to the kitchen.

"Daddy, you're staying too. It looks like we're gonna have a sleepover."

"A sleepover, Mommy?" EM asked. "I love sleepovers and Daddy is getting the movie. This is gonna be so much fun. We gotta make kettle corn, Mommy. We gotta get started now."

Magnus lifted his grandson. "Slow down, son. Tonight, we're gonna take the lead. Let's give Mommy a little break and you and I can make the corn. What do you think?"

"Sounds good to me, Grandpa."

"Mommy, you should go lie down now. We're gonna have tons of fun and the first one to fall asleep has the cooties."

Clarke smiled before kissing her son and mounting the stairs. She needed a glass of champagne and a bubble bath.

Chapter 8 – Twinning

Reshaunda Teal looked at herself in the mirror as the tears fell to her chest. Her reflection was just another reminder that the other half of her soul was dead. She missed her twin, and no amount of money could bring her back. Looking at herself was just like seeing her sister all over again and it broke her heart.

"Why did you leave me?" She asked her dead sibling. "I was getting myself together. Why couldn't you wait for me?" She screamed into the air. "I can't walk around here looking like you when you're not here anymore. It's too much. Why did you take her from me, God? She wasn't ready. I wasn't ready. I just need my sister back." Reshaunda cried as she fell to the floor in the bathroom.

Ree began to beat the cabinet doors, and before she knew it, she was throwing everything she could see. Her sister left her the condo and it took her four years to find the courage to live in it. Everything was the way Dee left it, and it only made Ree miss her sister more.

The news blamed the exploded car on faulty wiring and something with the gas tank, but everyone knew Dee was murdered. The streets didn't deny it, but no one was willing to point the finger. This was the thing that pissed Reshaunda off the most. The streets knew who killed her blood, but no one was talking. Four years of no answers from the police led this distraught young lady to seek answers on her own. Reshaunda was back in the Port City when that was the last place she wanted to be.

She couldn't stop herself as she continued to throw her sister's toiletries into the air. Finally, the cabinet was empty except for a small silver notebook. Reshaunda reached for the small book taped to the back of the cabinet. Her heart dropped as she read the first page.

Dear Ree,

If you are reading this diary, it means I am gone. You know there is no way I would have left you if I had the choice to stay. Clarke held me hostage in her home last night. I know she killed Mike, and she's afraid of what I will do. Ree, I know she'll come for me. They put me in charge of some dummy transaction with these Haitians, but I know it won't end well for me. If you find this book instead of finding me alive, start your search with Clarke and

Errol Bellow and the Port City Kings. Get some
justice for me, Sis. I know you can do it. I've
written everything down. Study it and do me proud.
I'm always in the mirror.

Love,

Dee

Reshaunda smiled. "I should have known you'd find a way to speak to me from the grave and don't worry, Sis. I got you," she spoke to the air.

Finally, Ree could get off the bathroom floor. She went for her cell phone and began to dial.

"Armon, there's been a change of plans. Meet me at Starbucks in an hour."

"What you mean, Ma?" Armon asked, feeling his control of the situation beginning to fade.

"I mean, if you wanna work with me have your black ass at Starbucks in an hour." Then the phone clicked, and she was gone.

***

Daddy, if I don't get a good cup of coffee, I'm gonna break something. Y'all have your reefer. I need my coffee and I need to get out of this house. It's been three days. Haven't you found out anything yet?"

"No, Babe. We're still working on it."

"Well, I need Starbucks, and I need it now," Clarke said pouting in front of her father.

"Come on, Baby. I'll take you." Magnus said, understanding that his daughter needed a break from the madness.

Magnus hit the button on the intercom system. "Black, bring the car around."

"Yeah, Boss," He responded.

Errol rounded the corner with EM on his heels. He'd been walking the chalk line ever since he'd come back home. Clarke wouldn't let him in the bed, but at least, he was at home with his family.

"You guys going somewhere?" He asked.

"Yep, I'm gonna make a coffee run with my Dad. Do you want anything?" Clarke asked.

"Mommy, Mommy, I want a piece of that lemon cake, okay?"

"You got it, Lil Man." Clarke smiled at her baby. She kissed him and then looked at her husband.

"Tell your Mommy we love her," he said to EM.

"Daddy and I love you, Mommy."

"I love you, too," she returned. "Are we ready, Daddy?"

"Yep, the car is outside, Baby."

He held the door open as his daughter walked through it, to the car.

Errol pounded the door with his fist as it closed.

"Daddy, why'd you hit the door? I know that hurt," EM asked.

"I'm gonna miss Mommy, that's all," Errol returned.

"She's coming back, right?" EM asked.

"You can count on it," he responded with a smile. "Mommy always comes back."

***

"Daddy, thank you. You are giving me life. I can't stand being cooped up in there like that. I thought I was gone go crazy"

"This life isn't easy, Baby and it isn't made for everybody. It gets tough sometimes."

"Yeah, Daddy, but look at everything I've done. You can't tell me that you ever thought your little girl would be a killer and to be completely honest, it all still bothers me at night."

"It's something that never quite goes away despite how deep you try to bury it, Clarke. The memory will never leave you. You have to change the way you think about it."

"I hear ya, but I can't help but think about the way Dee died. We were close. It didn't have to end that way, Daddy. We were wrong."

"You can't un-wreck a car once you crash it. The damage is done. You can't go back, Baby. Thinking you can do something to fix things will only make matters worse. You have to learn to make peace with your maker and throw your middle finger to the rest of the world."

The father and daughter ordered coffee, lemon cake for EM, and bagels for breakfast. Magnus rounded the corner to the drive-thru window when he slammed on brakes.

"What's wrong, Daddy?" Clarke asked, looking up from her cell phone. "You look like you just saw a ghost."

"I did. Look," Magnus said pointing at Reshaunda Teal.

"Oh, shit. I thought she was dead," Clarke said reaching for the door handle. "I have to speak to her. I have to know where she's been."

Magnus quickly grabbed his daughter's arm.

"Don't move, Baby," the concerned father responded. "We see them. They don't see us. That's a good thing."

"Well, I guess we know who Errol got the weed from," Clarke surmised.

"How could she pull that off?" Magnus asked.

"I taught her well and then she handled most of my business. I am not surprised. She was smart. Daddy, what are we gonna do?" Clarke asked. "She knows enough to get us all locked up."

"We are gonna stay calm and see where they go," Magnus returned as he handed the cashier money.

"Armon called me last week trying to make some money and we were supposed to meet but he canceled. I guess I didn't move fast enough, so he found another way."

"I guess so, too," Magnus responded as he took the tray of drinks from the woman in the window.

The duo watched Reshaunda and Armon talk in the parking lot for a minute before he returned to his car and the woman pulled out of the space.

"Hurry, Daddy. I don't want to lose her."

"Don't sweat it, Baby. I got it." Magnus returned.

He hit a button on his speed dial, and suddenly Rev. Dubois was on the other line.

"Meet me at my daughter's house in an hour. We got problems."

Reshaunda watched the all black Range Rover follow her to the entrance of her apartment complex. She looked into her rear view mirror as she turned, just in time to see the light hit the name of the tag in front of the car that'd been following her – Bellow 1.

Ree laughed out loud to herself as she spoke to a sister who was only there in spirit. "It seems we may have to enact our plan a little sooner than I thought, Sis,"

"Is she really living in the same apartment complex?" Clarke asked her father.

"It looks like it, Baby Girl. I'm gonna check it out, but for now, I need to get you home. I'll get some bodies together a little later."

"What am I gonna do with Errol?" Clarke asked her father.

"The man loves you, but he loves the game, too. You just have to find out which he loves most," Magnus said as he made a U-turn and headed back to the Bellow mansion.

"Mommy, Mommy, you're back," EM screamed.

"Yep, EM. I'm back. Mommy always comes back."

"What about Daddy?" The inquisitive toddler asked.

"Yep, him too. We will always come back for you," she answered.

"Hey, Grandpa."

"Did you miss us?"

"Yep, I've been thinking about that lemon cake since you left. Daddy even made me eat some oatmeal before you got back so I wouldn't have to wait."

"Here you go. You can have it now. Just go to the kitchen table with Tia. Daddy and I will be in there in a little while."

"Ok, Mommy. Do I have to give Tia a piece?"

"Of course, you do," Clarke laughed.

"Well, please tell her she can only have one piece because last time she had two, Mommy."

"Tia, I brought you back a piece of lemon cake as a surprise from EM. The rest is for him," Clarke said as she winked at her son.

"See, Mommy always has your back."

"That's right, Mommy. We stick together, and we don't keep secrets, right?"

"That's right, Lil Man. Now give me a hug and go have your cake," Clarke said as she leaned down to kiss her son on the forehead.

Errol swatted the boy on his bottom as he ran toward the kitchen.

Clarke looked up at her husband with a look only she and her father recognized.

"What's wrong, Babe?" Errol asked.

Clarke had no words for the traitor. Instead, she began to walk toward his office. He and Magnus followed.

Clarke walked to the bar and poured herself a drink. Magnus entered first, and Errol closed the door behind them.

"What's wrong, Clarke? What's going on?" He asked.

"The bitch isn't dead," Clarke answered.

"Wait, wait. Who isn't dead?" The confused man asked.

"Dee. She isn't dead. We just saw her at Starbucks with that young dude, Armon."

Errol fell into his chair. "What!" He exclaimed. "Are you sure?"

"Ummmmm, I'm pretty sure I know what she looks like," Clarke returned.

"Yep, that was her," Magnus interjected. "I'm not sure how she's been able to stay under the radar for so long."

"This hoe is even staying in the same apartment complex. She didn't even move," Clarke said nervously.

"That can't be right. We paid for her funeral, remember? Don't you think the funeral director would have told us if she was alive?" Errol added.

"Money makes the world go round. I have no idea what he did, but if you ever plan on getting into my bed again, you and your sidekick over there are gonna have to find out. Get rid of that bitch and for real this time or we're through."

"Do you hear her threatening me, Pop?" He asked.

"Yep and I don't blame her. You should have come to me. I could have gotten you what you needed without you forcing the family back in the game."

"I know Pop and if I could change things, believe me, I would."

"That dollar is late and short, Son. My daughter wants nothing to do with this life, but I'm sure you were aware of that. Now let me get this straight with both of you. I have created a very nice life for my family in a way that I prayed none of them would ever have to relive. I've paid my debts. I earned my respect and then here you come. First you defy me by sending for the shit when all you had to do was come to me and now your desire to "chief" has put my family back in harm's way."

"Tell him, Daddy," Clarke interjected.

"And you hush, girl. You should have been a ghost once you found out what this man was about, but you can't help who you love. I get that, but then you two dummies bring a child into the world without the common sense needed to protect him. Now, you have done well with EM and I'm proud, but this life is not for him and I'll see you both dead before we perpetuate another stereotype. So you two need to get your shit together and do it now. I am not having this conversation with either of you again. Next time, I'm taking my grandson and you two dumb asses can figure it out."

Magnus' tirade was interrupted by Tia on the intercom. "Mr. Magnus, you have a guest. Rev. Dubois is here

A surprised look covered Errol's face. "You brought that gun-toting preacher here?"

Magnus laughed. "Yep, that's my dude. He's my hidden hand. What's the problem, Son? Having flashbacks?"

"Nah, I've just never seen a preacher with a gun before." Errol smiled.

"I've had enough of this shit," Clarke said as she stood to her feet. "I'm not dealing with this. Oh, no! Mafietta has retired. I am Clarke Williams Bellow, future city commissioner and who knows, I may wanna be mayor or even governor. You are limiting my potential with this bullshit and I want out. I am not a fucking Soprano, and you aren't either. We have the cake, and we don't need this shit to survive. Stop selling us so short when there is so much potential for greatness here. Stop settling and Daddy, I love you, but if you take my son – you'll meet a side of me you never knew existed." Clarke walked over to her husband and mushed him in the face, "and the same goes for you too. Something ends here, Errol. You have to decide if it's gonna be your illegal dealings or your family. It's time you prove to me what's most important."

Clarke exited the room at the same time Rev. Dubois entered.

"Hello, Rev. Dubois. Welcome to our home."

"Thank you, Clarke. How's that little one?"

"He's growing so fast. I can hardly keep up. I'm gonna run to the kitchen and check up on him now. Good day to you, Reverend."

"Rodney, were you able to find out anything?" Magnus asked the preacher.

"Yes, I've checked Deshaunda Teal's birth and death certificates and guess what?"

"What?" Errol asked, already drawn into the conversation.

"She has a twin."

"A twin?" Magnus and Errol chimed in at the same time.

"Yep, it seems she was in a California rehab at the time of Dee's death, and she made her way back to the Port City about 6 months ago. We know she had over three million dollars in insurance benefits alone when she left Promises in Malibu. I would say that is more than enough to get a few pounds through the port. I even checked the records, and she was smart. The name says Lena St. John, not Lena St. James. She tricked your guys at the port with that slant on Lena's name."

"Are you fucking kidding me?" Errol asked.

"Nope, you guys have got to be more careful." Rodney Dubois responded.

"So what do we do now?" Errol asked.

"We make her an offer she can't refuse," Magnus returned.

"How? She has all the cards and plenty of money. She doesn't want more. She want's revenge."

***

Reshaunda Teal walked to her sister's cabinet and pulled out the small box filled with blunts and despite the voice from rehab reminding her to work through her issue, she lit one. She regretted her decision as soon as the smoke made its way to her head. Suddenly things became cloudy, and her clarity was gone. Her succinct and precise plan turned into something she'd never intended it to be.

Ree was in a rage. Seeing Clarke today almost made her throw up in her mouth. She'd only been able to read a couple of pages in Dee's journal before she had to meet Armon, but now things were clear. She didn't want to run their organization. She wanted to ruin their lives. She decided on pain. She would hurt each member of that family, and she would keep coming until there was nothing left.

She laughed as she thought of the Jay-Z line "Headshots, Nigga. Fuck your vest." She would cripple each of them, and they would never see her coming. The Bellows were so comfortable;

they were blind to the wolves and that's how she'd get them.

"Mommy, if I don't go outside, I'm gonna turn into a vampire," EM complained as he pulled at Clarke's pant leg. "Daddy, tell Mommy she's gotta let me go outside. I'm dying in here. Tell her, Daddy. Please."

"Come on Clarke. He's just a kid. Let him go out the back. Tia will be back there."

"Tia is not security. She's our housekeeper."

"Don't underestimate her. She can hold her own," Errol joked.

"This is our son we're talking about. We can't take any chances." Clarke interjected, not finding the humor.

"Believe me, Baby. If I had any concerns, I'd go out there myself."

"Yayyyy, Daddy will you go outside with me?"

"Yep, you got us into this, and you'll stand by your family while we get through it," Clarke blurted.

"Stand by me, Daddy. Let's go outside," EM chimed in, having no idea what he was talking about.

"Okay, okay. Let's go outside." With that, Errol grabbed his son's hand, and they headed for the back yard. "Stay out here with Tia for a second. I'll be right back." Errol advised the small one as he made his way to the bathroom.

"You want me to go with them?" Black asked.

"Yep," Clarke responded. "Be watchful, Black. My baby is out there."

"You got it, Boss," Black responded as he headed for the kitchen to reload his gun.

***

Armon's boy and his boy Stacy, parked a couple blocks away from The Bellow's home for days and nothing. That place was guarded like a fortress. The only hole in the Bellow's security was the maid, Tia. She went outside religiously every two hours to smoke her cigarette and she usually left the door open. Sometimes the kid would come with her but he always had Black following closely. The two waited patiently for a time when the minor was outside alone with the maid. That chance finally came.

Tia raised the cigarette to her mouth as the little one ran around her, alone.

"Yo, Son. Is that the kid and that maid right there?" Stacy asked.

"Oh shit, man. That's him" Armon answered.

Stacy and Armon had about two minutes to grab EM and get the hell out of there before someone saw or killed them.

"I don't know what kinda shit you got me into, A, but I'm not sure if I wanna be a part of this," Stacy answered.

"Wait, what the fuck do you mean?" Armon asked. "There has to be a way. This bitch paid us quite a bit of money to knock this family and we have to make sure it happens or we're next."

"This is a $100,000 job, and we've already gotten half, remember. You didn't seem to mind when you were flossing. We don't have time for second thoughts, Man. Let's get this job done and build our own empire. We can create our own Legacy. You can open up that barber shop you wanted, and I can finally open my restaurant. We can turn this around, man. It's just one job."

"Well, look. I can grab the kid, but that's all I can promise."

"Let's do whatever we can, Stacy and let's do it today. I have to have something to report to this woman before she puts a hit out on us both."

"Let's get 'em," Stacy ordered.

The two men exited their black Charger and crouched down as they headed to Errol's back fence. They moved like cats on glass as they walked through the brush and ended at the fence enclosing the Bellow's back yard.

"Ready, man?" Stacy asked his accomplice.

"Yep."

"Let's just start blasting on the count of three," Stacy replied. "One, two, three."

Suddenly shots rang out in Errol's back yard and he heard them as he opened the door. Errol quickly ran to his son and fell on top of him. In that split second, Errol saw every regret from his life pass before him. He saw his wife lying in a hospital bed. He saw when EM was born. He remembered his wife's pleas for a normal life and in this moment, all he could do was be a bullet proof vest for one of the best things that ever happened to him.

The back door swung open, and shots rang out from the Bellow's back door. It was Black. He ran the few yards over to Errol and EM and fired in the direction of the shots. He spotted two guys running. Then another shot rang out, and one of the kids dropped to the pavement. Suddenly the street was quiet again.

Black turned to find Clarke standing in the doorway, gun drawn. Within seconds, Black jumped the fence and walked over to the guy that was hit as he lay bleeding in the street.

"Who sent you?" Black asked.

Armon refused to respond.

"Oh, so you ain't gonna talk? Okay. We can do this the hard way then," Black said as he drug the shooter in the direction of the house.

Clarke rushed over to her husband and son. Errol was frozen. His hands gripped EM tightly. Clarke pried them away as her son screamed for his life. In that moment, everything she'd ever felt for Errol was gone. She grabbed her son and ran into the house where she locked the door.

EM screamed, "Mommy, Mommy what about Daddy? I want my Daddy. Let him in, Mommy. Let him in. I love him. Get my Daddy. Get my Daddy." The little one screamed as he tried to wrestle himself away from his mother to get to Errol.

Clarke felt daggers pierce her heart. This was the moment she'd always wanted to avoid, but now her husband's decisions finally followed them home. Her son's continued cries brought the mother back to reality.

"Look, EM. I need you to be a big boy. I need you to help Mommy. I'm gonna go check on Daddy, but I need you to go into the pantry with Tia and stay there until I come back."

"But, I want my Daddy. We need Daddy," EM continued to cry.

"I know Baby, but Mommy has to go make sure everything is okay first."

"I wanna help my Daddy," EM cried. "I wanna help too."

"Ok, here is what I need you to do. Take this phone and call Grandpa. Tell him there is a

Code Red and we need him and the crew here right now."

"Ok, Mommy. I got it," EM answered. "I'm strong, Mommy. I can handle this." The toddler said as he pushed out his chest.

A part of Clarke died that day as she watched her small child be forced into a life she never intended for him. EM was already bossing up, and that was just too much. She remembered her dead child and then looked over to the living one. This was it. Errol's ass had to go.

Clarke grabbed her Desert Eagle and headed to the back door. No one was in the back yard, but she heard screams from the basement. She descended the stairs and opened the door to find some teenage boy tied to a chair with blood and tears running down his face.

"Who sent you?" Errol asked.

"I ain't telling you shit," the little thug responded.

Black and Errol turned to Clarke as they heard the shot.

Reshaun screamed as the bullet pierced his knee.

"Wanna rethink that?" Clarke asked.

"Fuck, you," Reshaun returned as he spit blood from his mouth. Another shot rang out, and the captive screamed even louder as he felt the pain in his other knee.

"Next time I'm going for your balls," Clarke responded.

"You think I'm scared of some, Bitch?" He asked.

Black and Errol put their heads down and stepped aside as Clarke shot her family's assailant in the thigh.

"I'm not gonna miss next time," she warned.

"Woman, you're crazy."

"I've been called worse, now tell me who sent you or I'm just gonna kill you, and then I'll still find out, and when I do, I'm gonna kill them too," Clarke promised

"Okay, okay. It was Ree Teal."

"Ree Teal, who is that?"

"She's the twin sister of that lady who used to work for you. She's really got it in for you, too. There is a $100,000 price on your head right now, so kill me if you want. The streets ain't gonna miss that money, so if it wasn't me and my homeboy, it would have just been someone else."

"Where does this bitch live?" Clarke asked.

"I don't know," the prisoner responded.

"Call your friend," Clarke ordered.

"What friend?" He asked.

"Don't play with me, Lil Nigga. I heard two guns. Who was with you?" Clarke asked as she put the gun to Reshaun's head.

"It was Armon, Man. He brought me into this deal. I just wanted to get enough money to open my barbershop. That's it. I didn't know you were Mafietta. They didn't tell me that."

Suddenly, a large BOOM filled the air. Clarke turned to find Magnus holding a shotgun. He had a cigar in his mouth and never even dropped it. The bullet penetrated Reshaun's skull, and he was dead.

Magnus looked over to Errol. "Call a cleaner. I've already called my friends down at the precinct, and they are looking for Armon Smith right now. He won't make it through the night."

Clarke was filled with rage, and before she knew it, she'd turned it on to her husband. She stood with a gun at his temple.

"Look what the fuck you caused, Errol. Was it worth it? Was your green worth all this? Your son is hiding in the fucking pantry, probably traumatized and all because you wanted to get high. You disgust me, and you have disgraced me for the last time." Clarke looked over to her father, but never lowered the gun. "Daddy, get this nigga out of my house before I kill his ass, too."

Errol hung his head. He'd put the people he loved in danger, and while he would never give up on his family or let Clarke go, he had to play the game for now.

Magnus walked over to his daughter and slowly took the gun from her trembling hands. "This isn't the time for this, Baby. You and that man need to go into that house together and make sure my grandson is alright. He is the only thing that matters right now. Don't worry. Daddy has this under control."

Clarke allowed her father to take the gun from her hands, but then she began to pound Errol in his face and chest with her fists. "You lied to me. You are not who you said you were. I want a divorce. Do you hear me? I want a divorce."

Suddenly Errol had enough. He had almost lost his son, and he definitely wasn't about to lose his wife. He and Clarke took vows before God, and their marriage was forever. She and EM were his. He grabbed his wife and began to shake her. Within seconds, Magnus had him by the throat.

"Look here, Nigga. If you ever even touch my daughter again, you're a dead man. I know tensions are high, and our emotions are doing some crazy shit, but that's my baby, and if you hurt her, you'll answer to me. These motherfuckers got too close today, and it's time they pay. Now you two go see about my grandson."

Errol attempted to support his wife as they exited the basement, but she pushed him away. He'd pushed her too close to the edge, and he knew it.

Chapter 11 – Twisting the Knife

Clarke and Errol found their son sitting on a few cases of soda that Tia turned into a makeshift seat, eating chocolate chip cookies and wiping tears.

"Daddy, you're okay. Mommy went and found you!" The toddler smiled as he jumped into his father's arms. "I love you."

"I love you, too," Errol whispered through tears. He couldn't understand how someone so innocent and perfect could love someone like him.

Clarke walked over and kissed her son on the cheek. "Are you okay, Baby?" She asked.

"Yes, but Mommy what happened?"

Clarke swallowed hard. She wasn't prepared for that question. "I'm not sure, Baby."

"Daddy?" The little one asked, "Why were those men shooting at us?"

"Daddy doesn't know, but I promise you, I'm gonna find out," He said, patting his son on the back.

"I thought people were supposed to be nice to each other."

"They are, Baby."

"Then why did he shoot at us? He wasn't playing, Mommy. That wasn't a game. That gun was real."

"I don't know, Baby. I don't know."

"Well Mommy, guess what?"

"What, Baby?" Clarke asked, smiling at her child.

"I wanna gun."

"Why?" Clarke asked as her heart broke into even more pieces.

"I was scared because they had guns, so if I have a gun – I wouldn't have to be scared anymore," EM answered.

"Did you hear what your son just said?" Clarke asked as tears streamed down her cheeks. "Your son wants a gun. Do you see what you've done or does the bullet actually have to hit one of us for you to realize the danger we're in?"

"Clarke, I'm sorry. I never intended for this to happen."

"Don't you know the road to hell is paved with good intentions? It's a toll road that numbed a piece of my soul at every stop, and the bad thing is – you didn't even notice. Then as if that isn't enough, you corrupt our son, too? You have to go, Errol," Clarke ordered. "You have to get out of my house."

"No, Mommy. I want my Daddy. I'm supposed to have a Mommy and a Daddy. Not one, two."

"That's not your decision, Baby. We have to be safe," Clarke responded.

"Don't worry, EM. Daddy is not going anywhere."

"Shit, you say," Clarke murmured under her breath. "Let's go upstairs and play in your room." She said, looking at EM.

"Okay, but Daddy has to come." EM negotiated.

Clarke wanted to choke Errol, not play with him, but she obliged her son. "Only if you make me a promise."

"Okay, Mommy. What is it?"

"Promise me that you'll always be good."

"Cross my heart." The little one returned as he crossed his heart.

Clarke kissed her baby again and followed the duo upstairs to the playroom. She watched as Errol played the doting father with EM. She watched as he held his son close and answered his questions about guns. He made the entire situation very simple.

"We live a very good life. Your Mommy and I have worked very hard to make sure you have nice things and that's good. That's the way it should be, but then there are people who want all the things we have but who aren't willing to do the work it takes to get them. Sometimes these people may see something that someone else has and decide to try and take it instead or work for it. That's what happened today."

"Oh, man. They bothered us because they're poor, Daddy."

"They wanted something we have. Don't worry though. Daddy is gonna make sure it never happens again."

Clarke watched as Errol made promises he couldn't keep and it only made her more upset. What would he tell EM the next time something like this happened? How long could he keep lying to her baby before he figured things out or worse – what if EM wanted to take his place as head of The Kings?"

Clarke's morals had flown out of the window since getting with Errol, and she was beginning to feel heavy the repercussion of her choices. Clarke left the father and son and went to EM's room. She smiled as she saw all of the pictures her baby had taped to the wall. He loved his Mommy and Daddy. That was obvious. Clarke smiled as she walked to his closet and grabbed a small blue duffle bag. *He is one special little boy*. She thought to herself.

She began to stuff the bag with shirts, shoes, underwear, pants and a few stuffed animals. Then she dropped the bag down the laundry chute. She went to her room and did the same for herself. She knew Errol would never leave, but she would.

Clarke text her cousin Arvin, who'd arrived just after Rev. Dubois and her father. She hit the send button right as Errol came into the room.

"Who are you texting?" He asked.

"Don't ask me shit. I wouldn't know who I was talking to anyway."

"What does that mean?"

"It means that you aren't the man that loved his family so much that he was willing to change for it. It means you are just another selfish nigga who puts his wants ahead of the needs of everyone else. Someone shot at your family today and at your house. We have a son, Errol. Don't you think there's something wrong with this picture? This shit isn't okay."

"Don't you think I know that, Clarke? Do you think I ever meant for any of this to happen?"

"That didn't stop it, though did it?"

"Don't keep playing the victim with me, Mafietta. You are not innocent in this. You knew who I was when you married me, just like you knew who I was when you walked your little ass into my restaurant. You wanted a bad boy and you got one. Now you wanna leave because the kitchen got too hot? It doesn't work that way, Baby. This is forever."

"I'll love you forever. I can't deny that, but we can't be together right now. I need a break, and this is a prime time to take it. I'm leaving in the morning, and I'm taking EM.

"Like hell, you are," Errol returned. "You're not leaving me."

"I need a break, Errol. You're smothering me with this lifestyle, and I don't like who it forces me to become. Our kid just said he wanted a gun, so he didn't have to be scared. Does that not give your dumb ass a clue?"

"We can shelter him, Clarke. I'll just have to be more careful."

"That's the wrong answer, Errol. You have a choice to make, Mr. Bellow – your family or your lifestyle. EM and I are leaving, and you can get at us when you figure it out," Clarke said as she began to throw her toiletries in a small bag.

Errol grabbed the bag and threw it against the wall. "Do you remember what I told you when you wanted to call off the wedding?"

"I don't give a shit what you told me, Errol. We made a vow to God to protect our child and look what the fuck we've done. Why can't our past be enough? Why aren't we enough, Errol?

Why isn't your family enough?" Clarke half asked and half pleaded.

"I told you that I'd cut my baby out of you and throw your ass in the Atlantic Ocean, and I still mean that," Errol said, getting in Clarke's face.

"Oh, so you gone make me stay with you now? You gone hold me hostage?" She asked her husband as she stepped forward, closing the small gap between them.

"I'm saying that my family is staying together, and you can do so as my wife or as the woman locked in the fucking attic," Errol growled.

"You are crazy. I'm not staying here with you another minute. Have you forgotten who I am?" Clarke asked her husband.

"Try me, Clarke. I'm not letting you and EM go anywhere."

"Hard head makes a soft ass," Clarke said as she turned to head out of the bathroom.

Errol grabbed her arm and then pinned his wife against the shower door. "This is forever, Baby," He said as he forced his tongue into her mouth.

Clarke tried to push him away, but Errol didn't budge. He raised his hand to her chest and palmed her breast. "You're mine, Clarke. Don't forget that." He continued as he grabbed her ass and tried to slide down her jogging pants. Clarke freed one of her hands and slid it around her husband's waist as she allowed him to kiss her.

His anger relented. "I'm sorry, Baby. I promise it will never happen again. I'll never allow the street to come this close to you. Please forgive me and just let this go. I love you. I love my family."

Clarke knew better than to argue with her husband about a divorce. He loved her as best he could, but it was clear that he wouldn't let her leave. She was gonna have to run. She allowed him to kiss her again. Then she watched as he reached inside the shower to turn on the water.

She began to kiss her husband passionately, and he returned the gesture. Clarke pulled Errol's soiled shirt over his head and began planting kisses on his neck. He threw his head back and allowed his wife to rub his chest.

"Let's wash all of this bullshit away," Clarke suggested, opening the shower door. Errol entered first as Clarke grabbed the shower brush hanging from the hook on the wall. She quickly closed the door behind him, stuck the brush through the door handle, and ran for EM's room. It took Errol a few seconds to realize that his wife was gone and by that time, he was trapped in their shower stall away from his phone and the intercom system.

"Hey, Baby," Clarke said in a hushed tone as she reached EM's room. "Wanna go on an adventure with Mommy?"

"An adventure? Yayy!" The toddler shouted.

"Today we are gonna be superheroes. I'm Super Mommy, and you're Super Son are you ready?" Clarke asked?

"Yep, what are we doing?" He asked excitedly.

"Hold on to my neck and don't let go," Clarke instructed. EM grabbed Clarke's neck so tightly that it stunned her, but she was glad he was game.

She ran to the laundry chute in the bathroom. "You ready?" She asked EM.

"Yep, I'm holding on, Momma," the small one responded, ready for adventure.

Clarke took a deep breath and jumped into the chute.

EM screamed as he enjoyed the ride down. They fell to the bottom and landed on top of their laundry. Clarke moved quickly through the laundry room to the garage. The White Range Rover was running and she and EM jumped in.

Arvin was in the driver's seat. "Where are we headed, Cuz?" He asked as he raised the garage door.

"I need a spot under the radar."

"Gotcha, Cuzzo. Buckle up, guys," he said, looking at EM in the rearview mirror.

"Mommy is Daddy coming with us?" EM asked.

"No, he's coming in a few days," Clarke answered, unsure of what else to say.

***

Errol bammed on the bathroom door, but no one heard him. He tried using the various shampoo and soap bottles, but they just made noise. Clarke must be playing with me. He thought to himself. He sat on the bench made into the wall and waited. Minutes passed, and suddenly Errol jumped to his feet and began to pound the door. He knew exactly what was happening. His wife was leaving him.

Errol beat himself in the head as he paced the floor of the shower. His mind began to race and flashes of the last 6 years with Clarke flashed through his mind. He had to find her. If he could find her, he could make her see. He could make her see that their marriage and family were worth fighting for. Then the dark side took over. He saw flashes of her smile, her cleavage and then her extended arms. The only thing was, they were wrapped around another man. He sunk even deeper into despair as he saw the strange man pat his son on the head.

"Noooooo," Errol screamed as he thought of another man with his family. He balled his fist and pounded the frosted glass. The shower door shook the first couple of times, but slowly it began to crack. Errol ignored the blood running from his hands as he used both fists to fight the door. As his intensity increased, the crack in the door grew, and finally it shattered.

Errol wrapped himself in a towel and ran into the bedroom. He hit the intercom button. "Lock down the garage and don't let anyone in or out."

"Yeah, Boss," Black returned.

The King of the Port City Kings jumped into his Adidas sweats, slid into his shoes and ran down the stairs. He tripped over his feet several times on the way down the massive staircase as he screamed Clarke's name. In just minutes, he'd turned into a wild man.

"Where is my wife?" Errol screamed as he reached the bottom of the stairs.

Rocko and Black turned in awe from their post by the door. "We haven't seen her, Boss," Black answered. "What happened to you? Do you need some help?"

"No!" He yelled. "I need you two to do your fucking jobs and find my wife."

Errol let out a deep breath as he turned to climb the stairs. Maybe his misgivings were wrong, and Clarke was upstairs in EM's room. He turned on his heels and headed to the toy room. It was empty, so was EM's play room, Clarke's office, and the attic. His wife and child were gone, and it was all his fault.

Errol screamed as he ran down the stairs. "Get everyone in my office, now." The madman instructed as the blood dripped from his hands to the floor.

Magnus entered with the Reverend first, and Black and Rocko entered after.

"Where the fuck is my wife?" Errol asked as his hand pounded the desk in front of him.

"What do you mean, Youngblood?" Magnus asked.

"Clarke is gone and so is my son. Who helped her leave?" Errol asked as his eyes scanned the room.

"Do you mean to tell me that you lost my daughter and my grandson?" Magnus asked as his nostrils flared.

Rev. Dubois pulled out his phone and began to send a text. "I'm looking into it," he responded once his fingers stopped moving.

Errol started punching keys into his computer. He watched as the security images showed their white Range Rover leaving the garage.

"Damn!" He screamed. "She's gone. Black turn on the location device for the car," Errol ordered.

"Did you put her up to this?" Errol growled at Magnus.

"Son, I know you're upset, so I'll give you this one time, but if you ever talk to me like that again, it won't end so well for you," Magnus said as he stood to his feet and walked over to Errol's desk. "If she's gone, it's because you drove her away. I know you want your family back, but if you harm my child, I will murder your whole got damned family."

"Let's not get off track," Rev. Dubois interjected. "Where are we with the tracking device?"

"They're at Coldstone Creamery," Black reported. Then the entire room giggled.

"Damn man, my cousin escaped to get ice cream," Rocko laughed. "You must really be boring."

***

"You owe me ten bucks for getting under this car," Arvin joked after throwing the tracking device in the trash.

"Whatever, just get us outta here. Do you still have that beach house where you used to take your side chicks?" Clarke asked.

"Mommy, what's a side chick?" EM asked as he licked his cone.

"Ummm, well, baby . . ." Clarke began.

"A side chick is a girl that you like but who isn't cool enough to meet your Mom," Arvin advised.

"Oh, that's what you do with the Mud Ducks?" EM said without taking his eyes off the cone. Laughter filled the car as Clarke and Arvin laughed at the small one's view on side chicks.

The trip to Kure Beach was a pleasant one. The trio laughed and joked the entire way, seemingly as a way to forget the madness they were leaving behind. They had so much fun that they didn't notice the small Benz following them.

***

"What are the chances of this?" Stacy exclaimed. Reshaunda hadn't been very happy with the failed drive by and she even had some big guy rough him up a bit. This was just the break Stacy needed to get back into Ree's good graces.

He followed the car as it passed through Carolina Beach and kept going. He finally grabbed his phone and dialed his boss lady.

"What do you want?" Reshaunda asked.

"You'll never guess who I'm tailing," he offered.

"Why would I care who you're following?" She answered, unable to hide her annoyance.

"I'm trailing Clarke and her son." The excited youngster reported.

"Don't lose them. Which direction are you headed?" Ree asked with her interest peaked.

"We're headed towards Kure Beach," Stacy responded.

"We're coming that way. Just keep me posted," the anxious one responded.

***

"Something's wrong, Boss," Black reported.

"Whatcha say?" Errol asked.

"It's been an hour, and they're still in the same spot. I think they took off the locator."

"DAMN IT!" Errol screamed. "You gotta find her, Black. You gotta find her. I won't make it out here without my wife," Errol began to whisper as he put his head in his hands.

"Give her some space, Youngblood. She'll come around," Magnus predicted.

"I am scared to death for her. She's not safe." Errol finally confessed. "Just bring her home to me. We don't have to speak. I just need her home."

"Is there any other way to locate her?" Rocko asked.

"Nah, her car and cell phone are all I got and her cell's powered off. I don't have anything else.

"Yes, I think there is a way." Magnus smiled, pulling out his smartphone.

***

"I got the address, Boss. It's 444 North 4th Avenue," Stacy reported

"Thanks. Now you can leave," Reshaunda reported.

"Don't you want me to stay behind just in case they leave or something?" Stacy asked.

"Nah, you've done quite enough already," Ree responded. "We're gonna take it from here. All I need is two clean shots."

"You aren't gonna kill the boy, too are you?" Stacy asked.

"Yep, and I'm gonna do it first, just to watch her suffer!" She screamed.

"Well, that's cool and all, but now that I've delivered Mafietta, when can I get my bread?"

"Nigga, fuck your bread," she screamed. "My deal was with Armon. I don't even know your scrawny ass."

Stacy hung up. This shit was going too far, and he had to get things under control before the Port City Kings came for him, too. If she was gonna hold his cake, he would just get it from somewhere else.

He had to make a couple calls to get to Black, but finally, the deep voice was on the other end of the phone line, and he did the only thing a bitch ass nigga in his place could do, he sang like a bird.

"I'm sorry. I didn't know she wanted to start killing people. He commented, "And I certainly didn't know it was y'all. I'll show you where she lives and everything. I just need you guys to give me a pass. Don't put me down. I didn't know."

"Put a bullet in her head and I'll pay you the money," Black advised. "When is she gonna make her move?" He asked.

"She's headed that way now," the snitch explained.

"Well, I'll tell you what – you'd better be there to catch the bullet, or we're coming for your entire family. Do you understand? You and Armon were born and raised in the Port City just like your grandparents, and we can find them all. Fix this or you're gonna lose more than the investment for your business."

"Let's rock y'all," Black yelled into the intercom.

Suddenly everyone in the house scurried to grab their pieces. Magnus and the Reverend left first. They were followed by Black, Errol, and Rocko. Admiral and Lil' Stupid got the text and were already on their way.

Errol saw life with his wife pass before his eyes, and he couldn't help but blame himself for their current catastrophe.

Suddenly his phone rang. Errol answered nervously. "Hello?" He asked, but there was no response. He listened to muffled sounds and then he heard his wife.

"I don't care what you do to me, but if you harm my son, I will kill your bitch ass from the grave," Clarke screamed. "Put him in a room and give him his toys. This has nothing to do with him. This is between you and me."

Errol became enraged as the violent exchange filled the car speakers. Black put his head down as he heard the Boss Lady he'd come to love, plead for her son's life. Then he heard gunshots and screams. Then the phone went dead.

"Can't you get there any faster?" Errol asked, almost pleading.

"What will we do if they hurt her?" Errol asked his lifelong friend.

Black looked at his friend. "You already know."

Chapter 12 – The Aftermath

Errol heard the alert as it came over the scanner, but the police were still enroute. The house was dark, and there didn't seem to be any movement. Black and Errol went around back to look through the windows. Magnus and the Reverend went to the front.

Magnus could see EM on sitting on the bed watching television. He knocked softly on the window, trying to get the small one's attention. The TV must have been pretty loud because he never turned toward the sound. The determined grandfather knocked again, but harder. This time, EM looked, but as he stood, Magnus saw the rope wrapped around his leg.

That bitch had tied his grandbaby to the fucking bed. Suddenly, he couldn't wait to kill Reshaunda Teal just like he'd killed her sister. Magnus didn't care about the noise. He broke the bedroom window and rushed to his grandson. By the time the reinforcements came to attend to the noise, Magnus and EM were together in the closet. Rev. Dubois had no problem dropping each of the perpetrators.

"All clear," He yelled as a signal that Magnus and EM could leave their hiding place in the closet. Magnus rushed his grandson out of the window he'd used to enter the room, and they headed back to the car.

"This has been one crazy night, Grandpa," EM remarked.

"Tell me about it."

"When can we go home?" The little one asked.

"It's almost time. We have maybe another hour here, and we're gonna blow this whack place ok?" Magnus looked to his grandson for some indication of approval.

EM smiled. "Ok, Grandpa. So, what's next?"

"For now, I need you to lock the doors and just lay low for a second. Your cousin Rocko will take you to grab McDonald's. So, stay here, lay down, and don't move. I don't want anything else to happen to you," Magnus explained.

***

Errol could hear Clarke's screams from the steps of the seemingly dark basement. Each yelp made him want to die. She was being tortured, and it was all his fault.

"We can't go down the main stairs, Boss. They'll see us. We have to go in that side window. That backdrop will give us cover, and we'll be fine as long as we don't make any noise. The room was empty except for Clarke, Reshaunda Teal and some heavy guy they'd seen around town named Trainwreck.

Errol cringed as this monster punched his wife in the face like a man while that Dee look-a-like stood there with a gun pointed at her. "Call the Reverend to go to the window. He's a sharpshooter," Errol advised.

The truth was, he didn't know how to handle this. Love made Errol crazy. He couldn't envision life without Clarke. The thought of it took his breath and reminded him of the darkness that surrounded him before Clarke came into his life. If it were anyone else, he'd have taken the shot, but he couldn't risk that with his wife.

Errol stood paralyzed as Black called the Reverend. The call came just in time. He watched in shock as the big man drew his hand back and literally knocked his wife unconscious. Then the abuser looked to his boss.

"Let me have her. I'll kill her when I'm done," he told the woman beside him.

Reshaunda smiled. "I don't care what you do with her, but I want her dead in an hour. Oh, and her son has to die first. She has to watch. It's time this bitch really understands what it means to suffer. Go get the boy."

Clarke opened the one eye that wasn't swollen shut. She shrieked as the bullet sailed past her and into Reshaunda's chest. She watched the woman spit up blood before falling to the floor. Seconds later, Trainwreck returned. He looked at Reshaunda dead on the floor.

"Well, aren't you the resourceful one? Tell me how you did it? How'd you kill her?" The man asked.

Clarke's face was sore and swollen. She could taste the blood in her mouth and she refused to speak.

"Cat got your tongue?" The psychopath asked as he moved closer to Clarke. "It's okay, pretty lady because now you are gonna suck me off like your life depends on it because actually, it does," Trainwreck laughed.

Clarke watched as the man suddenly fell to the floor. Finally, she could let out a sigh of relief.

Errol rushed to her side. "Baby are you alright?" He asked as he removed the tape and socks from his wife's mouth. He tried to hide his disgust as he saw the bruises now covering her face. He untied his wife with sure hands and quickly lifted her up.

Her legs hung limply over his arms as she lay there fighting unconsciousness. Clarke began to come to as Errol rounded the house. Admiral came from the front door. "It's empty," he reported as two police cars arrived. Clarke opened her eyes for a split second but didn't have the energy to keep them open. Magnus spoke to the detective and as usual, he had everything under control.

EM sat in the back of Magnus' jeep watching Netflix on his Grandpa's tablet as he waited patiently for his parents. He was satisfied that he could see his Daddy holding his Mommy. She was sleeping, but he was glad his parents were together.

Errol approached the back window of the SUV and opened it. "How are you EM?" Errol asked.

"I've had too much ice cream, watched too much TV and I got shot at, but I'm fine, Daddy." The very intelligent child answered. "Is Mommy sleeping?" He asked.

"Yes, she is. Now let me get both of you home and put you to bed," Errol responded.

Clarke opened her eyes, but no words had yet come from her. Her eyes were so far away. Errol didn't recognize them anymore, but he knew this wasn't the time to antagonize his wife. He would be quiet, but the King knew he'd eventually have to face the aftermath of everything that had just happened.

Errol and Magnus tried to engage Clarke on the way home, but she sat in the front, refusing to move or speak.

"How are you feeling, Babe?" He asked.

Clarke looked at her husband with a blank stare and then turned her head back toward the window. Magnus tried to lighten the mood from the back seat as he and EM entertained each other. She heard her son's laughter, and that was the only thing that kept her from completely breaking down.

Mafietta was dead. She didn't want anything else to do with her husband or this life. She'd had enough. Enough of the guns around her child and the entire gangster mentality. Despite the way she was raised or what her father may have chosen as a career, at the end of the day, it had nothing to do with her. There was a reason Magnus kept her away from the life. Clarke sat in the seat trying to ignore the annoying pains coming from her face. She could tell it was still swelling.

Clarke reached for the visor and Errol touched her lightly. She began to scream. "Stop it. Don't touch me. Stop it. Just stop it!" She screamed.

Magnus hung his head as he saw the toll this life had taken on his daughter and in that moment he knew he would do anything he could to help her escape Errol and the Port City Kings.

"I just thought you might want to rest or let some of the swelling go down before you take a look at yourself," Errol whispered, not sure how to reach the love of his life.

So, now I have a broken face to match my broken spirit. Clarke thought to herself, still refusing to speak.

Errol drove home in silence, thinking of ways to reach the only woman he ever loved. The couple reached their home, and the husband heard as Clarke exhaled.

"EM has fallen asleep. I'm gonna take him up to his room and put him to bed." Magnus advised as he opened the door and left his baby to talk with her husband.

"You gotta understand, Clarke. I just wanted the best for my family," he said quietly.

He waited for a response from his wife, but again, she said nothing.

She looked at the bruises on her arm as they turned from red to purple, black, and blue and for the first time since her screaming, she spoke.

"Look at me, Errol. Look at all these bruises. Look at my swollen cheek and eye," she said, turning to her husband.

"Do you see what they did to me?" She whispered. It hurt to open her mouth and she could still taste the twang of blood.

"I'm so sorry I couldn't get there sooner. I searched the house for you, but you were gone. Where were you going, Clarke?" Errol asked, still trying to figure out how she'd gotten past his entire team.

"I was leaving you," she spoke gently, but the words hit Errol like a ton of bricks.

"Leaving me?" He asked as a tear hung on his eyelash.

"Yes, Errol. I was leaving you. Trouble follows you, Errol Bellow and I can't hang anymore. Your Mafietta is dead, and so is our marriage.

"Clarke, you can't mean that."

"Can't I?" She asked fighting the pain it took to speak. The woman held the side of her jaw hoping to minimize the pain as she continued.

"Look at me," she ordered, and her husband slowly turned to see a face he barely recognized. Clarke needed a doctor. He knew it, and she did too.

"Maybe we should get you to a hospital," Errol offered.

Suddenly, Clarke saw her way to get away from her husband.

"You're probably right. I am pretty sure I have some kinda concussion."

Errol's heart broke as he looked at a complete stranger. His wife's alter ego was dead, and its passing left him with a void and a woman he no longer recognized.

"I'll take care of you," Errol promised, mostly trying to reassure himself. "I'll take you to the hospital."

"Fine!" Clarke answered. "I don't want you to stay once my father gets here. I need some time."

"But you're my wife," he interjected.

"Yep, I am, but do you see where loving you has gotten me? Is this what loving you looks like? Is it black and blue and all puffy?"

Errol couldn't answer the question, and it was beginning to hurt even more for Clarke to speak.

"Please take me to the hospital," Clarke asked.

"Sure thing, Baby," Errol responded, finally relieved that Clarke would let him do something to help her.

"I'll call and tell your father," Errol offered.

"I got it." The emotionless person answered. "I'll shoot him a text," Clarke answered. Then Errol watched as Clarke pulled her cell phone from the inside of her pants.

"Why is your phone in your pants?" He asked.

"I knew they wouldn't look for it there," she whispered as she text her father.

"I will murder anyone who hurts you. You know that, right?" Errol asked, trying to find his manhood again.

"Yep, I saw the bodies on the floor," Clarke said as she stared out of the window, refusing to look at the man she had to leave.

"We're gonna get through this," Errol responded.

"I know," Clarke answered as Errol pulled into the Emergency Room parking lot.

"Let me run and get you some help. I don't want you to walk, ok." Then the nervous husband jumped out of his Rover and headed to the hospital door.

Clarke looked at the man she used to love and rolled down her window. She felt she owed him something.

"I love the good in you, Errol Bellow," she attempted to scream as she fought the extreme wave of pain that shot through her face.

Errol smiled and blew his wife a kiss as he headed into the hospital.

Suddenly, Clarke's phone rang. It was her father.

"Where is Errol?" Magnus asked.

"He went in to get me a wheelchair. We gotta move fast. Where are you?"

"I'm pulling up now. Get out and go stand beside the dumpster. I'll be there in about 2 minutes. I have to weave my way through this entrance."

Clarke fought every pain in her body as she stepped from the SUV and drug herself to the dumpster. She never knew she could find such comfort from leaning against a cold dirty piece of metal. She closed her eyes and opened them again as her father pulled up.

She moved into the car as quickly as her pain would allow. She locked the door and looked to the Emergency Room entrance. She saw Errol exiting the building with a wheelchair being pushed by some man who looked like a nurse.

They watched in silence as Errol and the nurse headed to his car. Clarke's heart sank as she saw the hurt, and then rage that covered her husband's face when he reached the empty car.

"Are you sure about this, Baby?" Magnus asked his daughter.

"Yep, Daddy. I'm sure," she answered looking in the backseat. Clarke smiled as she watched EM sleep. "Let's get out of here."

The car pulled away, and Clarke watched in the rearview as Errol banged the hood of his car and covered his face with his hands.

***

Errol uncovered his face and his thoughts rushed to his son, EM. He jumped into his car and punched the gas pedal the entire way home. All he could think of was his baby. Anxiety overtook the King as he pulled into his driveway. He saw his brother Admiral and his nephew Lil' Stupid standing in the driveway.

He had barely thrown the car into park before he was opening the door.

"Is my son in there?" He asked, barely able to keep his breath.

"Errol . . ." Admiral began.

"No. Shut up. Don't tell me shit. Is my son in there?"

"No," Lil' Stupid said as he dropped his head.

Errol fell to his knees in the driveway and let out a scream that would have broken any man's heart. His family was gone.

Admiral rushed to his brother and lifted the man and his shattered soul, carrying them both to the door. It took everything Errol's brother had to hold back the tears, begging to spill over their dam.

"She knew who I was, Admiral. I didn't lie to her. She knew me. She knew this, and now she's taken my son. Find her. Find her and bring them back," he cried.

Lil' Stupid rushed to open the door and helped carry Errol to his office. They propped the limp body up in the chair, and both took seats in front of it.

"Wha you wan mi do, Boss?" Lil' Stupid asked. He'd spent the last few years heading up their legal enterprises and had done well at keeping his hands clean.

"Go get my wife," Errol growled as he sat up in his chair.

"Hold on, Bro. You have to think this thing through. That woman is broken right now, physically and mentally."

"That gave her no right to leave me. We're married. That's permanent. That's till death do us part."

"Duh, but don't you see that someone tried to kill her entire family during the course of a couple of weeks? You, Clarke, EM or all of you could have been killed tonight. You need to give that woman her space. Trust her to do what's right."

"She is my breath. I need her. I can't breathe, Bro. I need my wife. I can't breathe without her."

"I'm trying to sympathize, Bro – but you should just man up and lay in the bed you made. You pushed this woman to the edge, and now you're bitching because she needs some time. I'm not going to bother her, and I'm damn sure not going to look for her. As a matter of fact, I'm even more committed to getting our family out of this shit. It ain't worth it anymore. We have too much to lose."

"So, what the fuck are you saying, Bro?" Errol asked.

"I'm saying it's time to go legit. It's time to get our shit together, and I hope you know that's the only way you will ever get her back."

***

"He's gonna come looking for you," Rocko said as he handed Clarke, her ice pack.

"I know," Clarke answered.

"What you are gonna do?" He asked.

"You don't want to know," She answered, staring off into space.

"Clarkeeeeee, what does that mean?" Rocko inquired. "I don't like the way that sounded."

"I'm not so blinded by naivety anymore. He's ruined every chance I've given him to get it together. Then he puts us all in danger over some bullshit with weed. Marijuana, man. The shit will be legal in a couple of years. Why couldn't he just stick to the plan and wait? We were almost there, Rocko. Almost there and then he goes and throws me back into the fire, and this time with my son. There is no forgiveness for that."

"Clarke, you don't mean that."

"You'll never know what it was like when I held my dead child in my arms. I felt him turn cold and watched his little complexion get darker and darker. You know I showed our cousin Keera a picture and watched her cringe as she looked at my baby. Do you know what that felt like? I couldn't protect him. I couldn't save him. I was just stuck with the hand I was dealt. Well, I have a choice now, and I choose to protect my son."

"So what are you gonna do?" Rocko asked.

Then for the first time, Clarke said it out loud. She took a deep breath, "I'm gonna kill him."

About the Author:

E.W. Brooks is a North Carolina Native turned Author, Publisher, and Producer. Her first book series, *Mafietta,* was initially released in 2013. Brooks' current novel, **BLIND**, is the 4th installment in the series.

Brooks' writing ability has also led her to write a host of other books. She co-penned *Envy and Eye Candy 1 & 2* with Author Kinshasha Serbin.

Connect with the Author:

www.Mafietta.com

www.ewbrooks.net

Facebook
www.facebook.com/ewbrooks

Instagram
@ewbrooksbooks

Twitter
@Mafiettaishere

Email
ewbrooksbooks@gmail.com